Meri Mercer Doesn't lie, Mostly

by: Jan Fields
Illustrated by: Tracy Bishop

magic wagon

visit us at www.abdopublishing.com

Published by Magic Wagon, a division of the ABDO Group,
PO Box 398166, Minneapolis, MN 55439. Copyright © 2014 by
Abdo Consulting Group, Inc. International copyrights reserved
in all countries. All rights reserved. No part of this book may
be reproduced in any form without written permission from the
publisher.

Calico Chapter Books™ is a trademark and logo of Magic Wagon.

Printed in the United States of America, North Mankato, Minnesota.
102013
012014

 This book contains at least 10% recycled materials.

Written by Jan Fields
Illustrated by Tracy Bishop
Edited by Stephanie Hedlund and Rochelle Baltzer
Cover and interior design by Renée LaViolette

Library of Congress Cataloging-in-Publication Data

Fields, Jan, author.
  Meri Mercer doesn't lie, mostly / by Jan Fields ; illustrated by
Tracy Bishop.
    pages cm. -- (Meri's mirror)
  Summary: Meri wants to share her magic mirror with her friends,
so she has invited her whole reading group to a party--but when
nobody else can see Mary Lennox from The secret garden in her
mirror she has to lie and say she was making it up.
  ISBN 978-1-62402-009-4
  1. Magic mirrors--Juvenile fiction. 2. Truthfulness and falsehood--
Juvenile fiction. 3. Friendship--Juvenile fiction. [1. Magic--Fiction.
2. Mirrors--Fiction. 3. Honesty--Fiction 4. Secrets--Fiction. 5.
Friendship--Fiction. 6. Characters in literature--Fiction.] I. Bishop,
Tracy, illustrator. II. Title. III. Title: Meri Mercer does not lie,
mostly.
  PZ7.F479177Me 2014
  813.6--dc23
                            2013028878

Table of Contents

1

A Great Idea

All over Room Eight, small groups talked about books or read them aloud. Voices were quiet. Mrs. Miller was almost never cranky, but she didn't like loud indoor voices.

Meredith Mercer turned her attention from *The Secret Garden* and looked around the room. The classroom was made up of round tables with chairs instead of the rows of desks her mom said students sat in when she was young. Meredith didn't think she'd like having a desk that made you an island all by yourself.

She turned back to her reading group. She'd read ahead again over the weekend. It was hard to pay attention when her group was reading parts she already knew. Still, when her reading group stopped at a really exciting spot, Meri just had to know what came next.

Jasmine's head was bent over her book as she read aloud, "A broad window with leaded panes looked out upon the moor; and over the mantel was another portrait of the stiff, plain little girl who seemed to stare at her more curiously than ever." She stopped and looked up at David Boomer, passing the reading turn to him.

"What do you think 'leaded panes' are?" David asked.

"I looked it up yesterday when I got to that spot," Meri said. She opened her reading notebook and flipped pages until she found a note she had made. Then she read aloud, "A window having small panes of glass held in place by lead."

David looked confused. He held up his pencil. "Like this stuff in a pencil?"

"That's not really lead," Sonia Wilson said.

"It's called lead," David said.

"We didn't know the difference either," Sean said. "Then someone in second grade stuck Sonia with a pencil and told her she had lead poisoning."

"I was scared," Sonia said. "Then my mom told me it wasn't real lead."

"Lead is some kind of soft, squishy metal," Sean said.

David nodded and turned back to his book and read, "'Perhaps she slept here once,' said Mary. 'She stares at me . . . .'"

David stopped reading and his head popped up. "I want to make a prediction about the book. I think there's going to be a ghost in the house. It's going to be the girl Mary Lennox keeps seeing in the pictures. The ghost is the one crying."

Everyone wrote down David's prediction. Meri wrote it too, though she didn't think there was going to be a real ghost. The big house in the book was mysterious, but she didn't think it was haunted.

"Did writers put ghosts in really old books like this?" Sean asked.

"Sure," his sister answered. "Remember *A Christmas Carol*? It has ghosts and it was written a long, long time ago."

"I don't think I would like Mary Lennox," Jasmine said. "She's mean sometimes. She even called people names at the beginning."

"That's true," Meri said. "But she never really had any friends, and she barely saw her parents. And then she had to live with strangers at Misselthwaite Manor."

"Oh." Jasmine's eyes widened. "Maybe that's what the author was trying to do in the book. She's trying to show what happens when someone doesn't have any love." Jasmine quickly wrote that down in her reading journal.

Sean's nose wrinkled, and he poked at the book. "So it's a lesson book. I hate stories with lessons."

Meri wasn't sure. Almost all books had little bits of lessons, but *The Secret Garden* seemed to be about more than that. "It has good stuff too," she said. "Like this part where Mary's exploring the creepy house."

"It also had that snake in the beginning," David said. David liked books with animals in them, especially dangerous animals like snakes and sharks. "And I still think there's going to be a ghost."

She hoped David wouldn't be disappointed, but Meri still didn't think there would be a real ghost. She looked down at the pages of the book. Meri spoke very quietly, talking to herself. "I could ask Mary."

"Oh, what are you going to ask yourself?" Jasmine teased.

"Not herself," Sean said, "the book girl. Do you talk to your book like Sonia does?"

"I don't talk to books that much," his sister said, poking him in the arm. "Only during the really exciting parts."

Meri was glad when the twins teased back and forth and completely forgot about Meri's comment. She did talk to her book, in a way. Meri had a magic mirror at home. Whenever she left a book on her desk in front of the mirror, the main character appeared in the mirror. Meri thought it was the best magic anyone could ever have. The book characters helped her with hard problems sometimes.

Meri didn't like keeping the magic secret. She thought it would be great fun if her friends could talk to one of the book characters, too. She just didn't think they would believe her if she told them. They would think she was playing a trick. She would have to be able to show them, and the mirror was too big to bring to school. As she thought about ways to tell her friends about the mirror, David went back to reading out loud.

"It's your turn to read," David said when he finished.

Meri looked up sharply. She wasn't sure where David had stopped. She looked down at her book, looking for the place.

"Wow, Earth to Meredith," Sonia said, leaning over to point at the spot where Meri needed to read. "What were you thinking about so hard?"

"A party," Meri said as the idea popped into her head. "I want to have a party at my house, and I want you all to come."

"Will it be a girlie party?" David asked. "With dancing and messing with each other's hair?"

"No," Meri said, laughing. "We can watch a movie." She talked faster as an idea came to her. "I've seen a movie of *The Secret Garden* at the library. We can watch it together. That would be fun."

Sean nodded. "But we probably should finish reading the book first so we don't spoil it."

"Right, we'll have the party after we finish reading the book," Meri said.

"A movie would be fun," Jasmine said. "Like having the book come alive."

"We'd see what Mary really looked like," Sonia said.

"I don't know about that," her brother argued. "Sometimes they get the looks all wrong in movies."

Meri smiled as the twins argued. They never really got mad at each other. It reminded Meri of her own family. Someone was always squabbling at her house, but no one stayed mad for long. She was glad all her friends would get to meet her family. They would watch the movie together. And she would show them how a book really comes to life. Meri would show them all the magic mirror. They would see Mary Lennox for real.

"Well, if we can't have the party until we're done reading," David said, nudging Meri's arm. "Then you better start. It's still your turn."

2

Preparing for the Party

Meri finished *The Secret Garden* well ahead of everyone else. Waiting for them to finish seemed to take forever. She discovered that her favorite lines were even better when someone read them aloud. She found it hard to be patient during the parts that were not her favorite. Sometimes she had to wiggle in her chair to keep from telling them to hurry up.

Every day after school, Meri talked to her mother about the party.

"David likes hot dogs," Meri announced on Wednesday. "Can we have hot dogs at the party?"

"Sure," her mom said. "But you'll have to stop changing the menu soon. Once I buy the food, you're stuck with it."

"We don't mind being stuck with hot dogs," Meri said.

"Do all of your friends like hot dogs?"

Meri felt a pang of worry. She tried to picture each person's face when David talked about hot dogs. Did any of her friends seem to be thinking, yuck? "I'm not sure."

Her mom gave her a hug. "Why don't you just make a menu, then take it to your reading group and see if they all like most of the things. As long as you have something for everyone, it's okay if someone doesn't like one of the things."

That sounded a little confusing to Meri. As she stood there sorting it out in her head, Thomas and Kat raced into the room. The twins nearly body slammed Meri.

"Can we come to the party, too?"

"Not all of it," Meri said. "You can't follow us to my room or anything like that. But you can eat the party food."

"Yum!" Thomas and Kat sang out.

"And I guess you can watch the movie with us."

Thomas narrowed his eyes. "Is it a girlie movie with fancy clothes?"

"It's not girlie, but you might think the clothes are fancy," Meri said, then shrugged.

"If we start watching and you don't like it, you don't have to keep watching."

"We could watch a Harry Potter movie instead," Thomas suggested. "Then I know I'd like it."

"We're watching *The Secret Garden* because it's the book we're reading."

"There are Harry Potter books," Thomas said. "You could read one of those. You read really fast."

"We've already watched the Harry Potter movies a million bazillion times," Kat complained. "I don't want to watch them again. I don't want to watch a gardening movie either. That sounds boring. We should watch a movie with singing and dancing."

"Yuck!" Thomas howled.

Mom shooed everyone out of the kitchen. Thomas and Kat piled onto the sofa to argue about movies. It was an old argument, so Meri just shook her head and hurried upstairs to her room.

Meri slipped into her desk chair and stared into her mirror. She saw her own face. She knew that was normal, but Meri found it a little strange to look at herself in the slightly warped glass of the antique mirror. She had seen so many different faces there.

Meri wondered if she should go ahead and talk with Mary Lennox for a few minutes. She could tell Mary about her friends and about the party. Then Mary wouldn't be quite so surprised and might be nice to Meri's friends. She wasn't sure her friends would like her magic mirror as much if Mary Lennox was mean or called anyone a pig.

Meri dug her book out of her backpack. She placed her book carefully on the desk in front of her and watched the mirror.

Usually, she didn't look into the mirror while it changed. It was a little creepy to watch her own face turn into someone else's. This time she watched the mirror carefully. She reminded herself that this is what her friends would see on Saturday. At first, she peered into her own blue eyes and pushed her crazy curls away from her face.

Slowly, her face seemed to fade. At first it was just fuzzy, as if her eyes were watering. Then it grew more and more blurry. Her curls seemed to blend into the room behind her. It was like watching herself turn into a ghost. She could look right through her own body and see her bookcase crammed with books. Then slowly, the girl in the mirror became more and more solid, only she didn't look like Meri at all.

The girl in the mirror had long, yellow hair, only a little darker than Meri's, but her hair was straight as string. While Meri's face was round, the mirror girl's face was long and thin.

As always, Meri felt the thrill of excitement at seeing the mirror's magic. She'd loved books all her life, but now she could see her favorite book friends face-to-face.

3

Meeting Mary Lennox

The girl in the mirror stared at Meri. She leaned so close to the mirror glass that her nose almost touched.

"Hello, Mary Lennox," Meri said. "My name is Meri, too. Well, Meredith really, but everyone calls me Meri. I'm so glad to see you."

"Why?" Mary Lennox asked. She sounded really curious. "People never like me, and I never like people. Not when I first meet them, and usually not later either."

"I like you," Meri answered. "I think you're very brave. And I like that you never give up on things. I was hoping you would tell me all about the secret garden and about the manor."

Mary's eyes went wide. "How do you know about the secret garden? No one is supposed to know except Colin and Dickon."

"It's complicated," Meri said. "But I promise Colin and Dickon didn't tell me."

Mary frowned at her and crossed her arms. For a long moment she didn't speak at all. Finally she sighed and dropped her arms.

"I guess I am glad to have someone to talk with who knows the secret," Mary said. "Colin is so full of talk about his sickness, even though I don't think he's a bit sick really. And Dickon tells the most wonderful stories that sometimes I forget to talk at all."

"I would love to meet Dickon," Meri said.

"He's very interesting. Everything changed when I found the garden and met Dickon. The manor is a gloomy place," Mary said. "Though not so bad as it once was. The garden is growing, but it is still wild. I like it wild. Colin does too and so does Dickon."

"I wish I could meet them both," Meri said. "Does Colin go out to the garden yet?"

Mary laughed and her face brightened. "We push him in a big pushchair because he's never walked around in all his life. He's practicing though and plans to walk. The secret garden is magic, and it's making him well. That's what he says."

"It sounds wonderful. I wish I could go there."

At that, Mary looked around the mirror room where she sat. "Where am I? I've not seen a room like this at the manor. It's so small and plain. It's almost like a cottage room."

"This is my house. I have a big family like Martha does," Meri said, remembering the maid in *The Secret Garden* whose family came to love Mary Lennox so much.

"That must be grand," Mary said. "I'm all alone, and I used to be lonely. I don't feel a bit lonely now. I'm still alone, but I also have Colin and Dickon. I just realized Colin is my cousin, so he is my family. He is so funny and different, I hadn't thought of him that way. I think of him as a friend mostly."

"Friends are nearly as good as family," Meri said. "I want you to meet my friends. They're coming here to have a party. When they come, I'd like you to meet them."

"What are they like?" Mary asked.

Meri thought about each of her friends. "Jasmine is shy but very sweet. David is nice too. He thought there was a ghost at the manor."

"I thought there might be too," Mary said. "But it was only Colin. He cried, because he thought he was going to die. He doesn't think so anymore. He says he will live forever. That's almost as silly as thinking he would die. No one lives forever."

"It would be nice though," Meri said.

"Do you think so? I think I would get terribly bored."

"I never thought about it like that." Meri thought for a moment, and then shrugged. "My other friends are twins. Sonia tells the most wonderful stories. And Sean is so funny."

"They sound like two halves of Dickon," Mary said. "He tells wonderful stories, and sometimes he makes me laugh. He's Martha's brother, you know."

Meri nodded.

"Is the party a very long time from now?" Mary asked. "I don't think I would like to stay and wait very long. Colin needs me. He might forget that he's getting well if I stayed away too long. And we have so much work to do in the garden."

"I won't ask you to stay until the party. You'd be stuck in that mirror room the whole time."

"Oh! That's like when I first came to the manor, the housekeeper told me that my bedroom and the next were where I would live. She said I had to stay in them and not to forget that. I didn't forget it, but I didn't stay in my rooms either."

"I don't think I would have either," Meri agreed. "But I don't think you can leave the mirror room. I won't leave you stuck there. When we're done talking, I'll send you right back to the Manor."

"That would be best," Mary said. "We still have so much work to do on the garden. And I need to help Colin with his walking practice."

"You don't mind coming back for the party?"

"Not a bit," Mary said.

"Good." Meri carefully picked up her copy of *The Secret Garden*. "I'll see you soon then." She watched as Mary Lennox slowly faded away, and Meri Mercer took her place.

Meri's Surprise

Meri's reading group worked on the packet for *The Secret Garden*. Sonia was writing on the worksheets since she had the best printing.

"We still have to decide on how much we liked the book," Sonia said. "Should I color in all five stars?"

"No," her brother said. Everyone looked at him in surprise. "I liked the book, but it needed a ghost like David said. Why tell us all about the pictures of the little girl in the house if Mary wasn't going to see her ghost?"

"Maybe it was to make you think about ghosts," Jasmine said. "Then you might think all of Colin's noises were ghost noises. That way you'd be surprised when it turned out to be a normal boy."

"Thinking about a ghost isn't as good as having a ghost," Sean insisted. "And Colin isn't exactly normal."

"But he becomes a normal boy," Jasmine said. "After Mary helps him. I don't think it really needed a ghost with all the good stuff it had in it."

"It didn't need a ghost, but having a ghost would have been good," David said. "But I think all the animals made the book five stars. Wouldn't it be great to be able to talk to animals like Dickon?"

"That was a good part," Jasmine agreed. "I loved it when he brought all the animals in to see Colin. That helped him get well too, I think."

"So," Sonia said, "how many stars? I vote five."

"Five," David said.

"I think five," Jasmine added.

Sean crossed his arms. "Four. It should have had a ghost."

"How about four and a half?" Meri suggested. "That would be more than four but less than five. Would that be fair?"

"I guess," Sean grumbled.

His sister grinned at him. "I think for the next writing prompt, you should write a story with a ghost in it."

David held up his copy of *The Secret Garden*. "Should we turn in our books?"

"I guess," Jasmine said. "Since we're done with them."

"Wait," Meri said. "I have an idea. Why don't we bring them to the party at my house? We can put them in one of my mom's baskets and use them for a centerpiece on the table."

"That sounds good," Jasmine said.

"Yes, let's be sure to have lovely décor," Sean said, using a silly voice. "And we should put flowers in the basket, too. Don't you think so, David?"

David used a silly voice, too. "Yes, that will be too marvelous."

"Don't tease," Sonia scolded as she carefully colored in the stars. "So, when is the party, Meri?"

"On Saturday. I have invitations in my backpack. I'll give them out at lunch."

"Saturday?" Jasmine said. "Isn't it supposed to snow on Saturday?"

"It was supposed to snow last Saturday," Meri said. "But it didn't."

"And I heard it was supposed to snow yesterday," David said. "But it didn't."

"My mom says that Connecticut weather is contrary," Meri said. "Just like Mary Lennox in the book. It hardly ever does what it's supposed to do, so they have to say 'snow' when it's winter, just in case."

"I wish it would snow," Sonia said. "It never snowed where we lived in California. We thought it snowed all the time in Connecticut."

"It's not even really winter yet," Jasmine said. "It doesn't become really winter until the middle of December. This is just the beginning. I'm sure you'll see lots of snow this winter."

"I hope so," Sean said.

"Hey, if it snows at the party, we can slide down the big hill in your backyard," Jasmine said, her eyes shining. "That looks like a great snow hill."

"It is," Meri said. "And we have lots of snow saucers and stuff for sledding."

"As long as it doesn't snow before the party," Jasmine said. "Then my mom probably wouldn't take me. She doesn't like to drive when it's snowing."

Meri didn't think they really needed to worry about snow. She hoped not anyway. She wanted to see their faces when Mary Lennox appeared in the mirror and talked to them. Sean could even talk to Mary about ghosts, if he wanted. She giggled a little as she thought about it.

"What are you laughing about?" Sonia asked.

"Nothing," Meri said. "I was just thinking about the party. I have a surprise to show you guys."

"Is it food?" David asked. "Like a cake?"

"No cake," Meri said. "But my mom's making brownies."

"Yum," Sonia said. "Is that the surprise?"

"No, it's not a food surprise," Meri said. "It has something to do with the book."

"We already know about the movie," Sean said. "Or is the surprise that we aren't going to watch the movie?"

"We're going to watch it," Meri said. "I'll go and check it out tomorrow at the library. If you check it out on Friday, you get to keep it all weekend."

Sean narrowed his eyes. "Is it some kind of dress-up game? I really don't want to dress up in funny costumes and pretend we're in the book."

Meri laughed at that. "That sounds like fun, but I don't have costumes. We're not dressing up."

Both David and Sean sighed in relief.

"Is it prizes?" Jasmine asked. "Like goody bags?"

"We are going to have goodie bags, but that's not the surprise."

"Well, I can't guess what it might be," Sonia said. "So it'll have to be a surprise."

"A big one," Meri said, and she smiled a small secret smile.

A Crazy Party Game

Just as Meri expected, it hadn't snowed a single flake when she got up on Saturday morning. She hopped out of the bed. Then, she made her bed neatly. She didn't want her room to look sloppy when her friends came.

She rushed to the bathroom, and then got dressed. When she finished, she checked her clock. She still had hours and hours before her friends would be there.

Meri hopped down the stairs. Her mom was cooking oatmeal on the stove. "You're up early," she said. "Did you hear anyone else rustling around yet?"

"No," Meri said. "Do you need me to clean anything for the party?"

"It's all clean," Mom said. "Though you can help with the dishes after breakfast. Are you ready for some oatmeal?"

Meri nodded. She liked her mom's oatmeal. It was fluffy and buttery. And her mom always added a drizzle of maple syrup to each bowl.

After breakfast, Meri spent all morning pacing. When she saw someone put something down, she scooped it up and put it away.

"Meri, stop it!" Thomas yelled at her. "I was playing with that stuff."

"You left it in the living room," Meri said. "You weren't in there."

"I was going to the bathroom!" Thomas yelled. Then he stomped up the stairs to get his toys again.

"You are acting a little crazy," her older sister Judith said from the sofa, where she was curled up with a book.

"I just don't want things messy," Meredith said. She frowned at Judith. "Do you think you should have your feet on the sofa?"

"This sofa is old and ratty," Judith said. "My feet aren't going to hurt it. We always put our feet on the sofa. You put your feet on the sofa."

"Not today," Meri said.

"Okay, that's it," Judith said. "I'm going to the high school to watch Hannah's ball practice. It's got to be better than watching you play Captain Clean." She walked to the stairs and yelled, "Thomas, Kat, do you want to go watch Hannah's practice with me?"

"Yeah!" The twins thundered down the stairs and straight outside. Judith had to call them back in for coats, scarves, and boots. Finally they were ready and left to watch their oldest sister's basketball practice.

After that, the house stayed neat, but Meri didn't have anything to do. She tried to settle down with a book, but the words just seemed to bounce off her brain.

When she heard the first knock on the door, she rocketed off the sofa so fast, she tripped over her feet and almost fell down.

"Easy, Meredith," her mother said as she walked through to get the door. "You certainly are wound up."

Meri took a deep breath and followed her mother to the door. When she opened it, they saw Jasmine. She was grinning and clutching her copy of *The Secret Garden*.

"It didn't snow," Jasmine half shouted.

"Yet," Jasmine's mother said, giving the sky a worried glance. She shifted Jasmine's baby brother to her other hip and shook hands with Meri's mom. Then, they all came in the house.

"I love your house," Jasmine said. "It looks so comfy."

"It's certainly lived-in," Meri's mom said, with a laugh.

The two moms chatted until the baby began to fuss. "I should get him home. He needs lunch and a nap. Do you think the weather is going to be okay for this party?"

"I'm sure it'll be fine," Meri's mom said. "If it snows, Jasmine can stay until it stops and the plows go through."

Jasmine's mom looked relieved. "Thanks." She hugged Jasmine and left. As they were waving good-bye to her, a van pulled up. Sonia and Sean piled out and ran up to the porch. They each carried a copy of the book.

"We're here," Sean said. "The party can begin."

"You must be Sean," Meri's mom said.

Sean and Sonia's dad stepped out of the van but didn't come up to the porch. He just waved and yelled, "I'll be back to get them this afternoon!"

"That'll be fine," Meri's mom yelled back. "Now, everyone in the house. We don't need to heat the outdoors."

David came soon after that. His dad came in for a few minutes but didn't stay long. Meri saw her friends all carrying their books.

"You can just put your books on the piano," she said. "Mine is upstairs."

"So," David said, "are you going to show us the surprise?"

"Yes," Meri answered. "It's up in my room."

They trooped noisily upstairs. Meri's heart was pounding so hard she was surprised no one asked what the noise was. She was about to share her biggest secret in the world with her best friends.

When they walked into her room, she pointed at the mirror. "My Aunt Prudence

sent me that mirror for my birthday."

"Wow, it's so old looking," Sonia said. "It makes my face look spooky. Hey, Sean, look at you. You look like a ghost."

The rippled glass did make reflections look odd when Meri wasn't using the magic.

"Is that the surprise?" Jasmine asked, disappointment thick in her voice. "I've already seen your mirror. It's nice, but it's not a big surprise."

"There's something you don't know about the mirror," Meri said. "It's magic."

"Magic?" her friends said together. Then they looked at each other and laughed.

"Is this a game?" Sonia asked.

"No, it's real magic," Meri said. She put her copy of *The Secret Garden* on the desk near the mirror. "Now watch the mirror."

Everyone stood silently, eyes intent on the mirror. Meri saw her image begin to fade. "It's starting," she said. The image grew more and more dim.

Her friends began shifting behind her. She guessed they must be shocked by seeing Meri fade out of the mirror. Then slowly Mary Lennox appeared. She smiled at Meri.

"There," Meri said, pointing at the mirror. "What do you think?"

Her friends peered at the mirror. Finally David said, "I think you have nice curls?" As soon as he said that, his cheeks flushed, and Sean poked him.

"What?" Meri turned back to the mirror. Mary Lennox looked around at her friends from the other side of the glass. "Don't you see that?"

"We see a mirror," Sean said.

"And our reflections," Sonia added. "Were we supposed to see something different?"

"Mary Lennox!" Meri said. "She's right there."

Her friends looked into the mirror, then turned to look at Meri. "Is this some kind of game?" Jasmine asked. "Because I don't really understand."

"You don't see her?" Meri asked weakly.

"They do not seem able to see me," Mary Lennox said. "Though I see them. Some of your friends are quite brown. Are they from India?"

"No," Meri said. "They're from my school."

"Who are you talking to?" Sean asked, then he laughed. "This is the weirdest game ever."

Snow!

Meri looked at each of her friends in stunned disbelief. They couldn't see Mary Lennox in the mirror. They really couldn't see her.

"She's right there," Meri whispered.

Sean leaned so close to the mirror that he was almost rubbing noses with Mary. "That's amazing. From this angle, she looks exactly like me."

"I do not," Mary Lennox said, stomping her foot. "I don't look anything like that boy."

David laughed. "Is this some kind of pretend game?"

"Can't you hear her?" Meri asked. "She's there. She's right there."

"If this is a game, it's not much fun," Jasmine said. "I think you should quit."

"Yeah," Sean agreed. "When a trick doesn't work, it doesn't get any better if you keep pretending it did."

"You don't have to make stuff up to get us to like you," Sonia said. "We like it better when you tell the truth."

"Playing pretend isn't lying," Jasmine said loyally. "Not really."

"It is exactly like lying," Sonia said, "when you insist it's real."

"I don't think you should call Meri a liar," David said, frowning at Sonia. "She's just playing a game, right, Meri?"

"Right," Meri said weakly. She didn't want her friends to fight about her. They really couldn't see Mary in the mirror. Maybe the magic only worked for Meri since the mirror was her present. She sighed. It would have been nice if Aunt P had included some kind of owner's manual with the mirror.

Meri looked around at her friends. They were all looking at her with worried eyes. Meri forced a laugh. "It was a silly thing to pretend."

"What are you saying?" Mary demanded from her side of the mirror. "You know I'm not pretend." She tapped the mirror from her side and Meri could hear the soft thud of her finger against the glass.

No one else turned toward the mirror. No one else could hear it. Mary stomped her foot again. "Why are you lying to them?"

Meri looked at her and shook her head. She was not going to be seen talking to a mirror.

"Well, that's okay," Jasmine said. "We'll just go watch the movie. Then we'll all see Mary Lennox."

"What's a movie?" Mary asked. "How will you see me if you're going somewhere else?"

Again Meri ignored her, though she hated to do it. She reached out and took the book from the top of the desk. "Yeah, we should go watch the movie."

"Why are you ignoring me?" Mary demanded with another stomp of her foot. "You said you wanted to be my friend!"

Meri felt a sick knot in her stomach. She did want to be Mary's friend. But she didn't want to lose her only school friends. The mean girls in her class already said she was weird. She didn't want her friends to think so, too. As she turned toward the door, she could see that Mary was already fading in the mirror.

"You're acting mean!" Mary shouted, her voice hollow.

Meri knew it was true.

The group walked down the stairs quietly. Jasmine kept sneaking nervous glances at Meri. Meri smiled back each time, even though she didn't feel at all happy. As she walked, she wondered if maybe she had imagined the story people in the mirror all this time. She didn't think she had a wild imagination. You'd have to have a wild imagination to see someone in a mirror who wasn't there.

At the foot of the stairs, Meri dropped her book on the stack teetering on the old piano. Then she called out toward the kitchen, "We're going to start watching the movie."

"Okay," her mom called back. "I'll bring the popcorn."

"Popcorn!" David said. "Yum."

They piled on the old sofa and the overstuffed chair that sat next to it. Meri held up two movie boxes. "The library had two versions. One from 1949 and one from 1987. Which do you want to watch?"

"Not the one from 1949," Sean said. "That will be in black and white. Those movies are boring."

"But it's closer to the time *The Secret Garden* was written," Jasmine said.

"A little," Meri said. "*The Secret Garden* was published in 1911. It says so in my copy at the front."

"Wow, that's more than 100 years ago," Sean said. "No wonder it has so many weird things. Still, I don't want to watch a movie without color."

"Okay," Meri said. "We'll watch the 1987 one." She slipped the movie into the slot on the player, then scooted back to lean against the sofa.

"You can sit up here," Jasmine said, patting the sofa cushion beside her. "We'll squish up."

"No, that's okay," Meri said. "Sometimes the library movies have fingerprints or scratches. If I sit down here, I can get to it quicker."

She also wasn't sure she wanted to sit close to her friends. She understood that they couldn't see Mary. But she was still a little mad that they didn't believe her. She knew that wasn't fair, but she felt it anyway.

The movie was nice, but Meri couldn't help thinking that the girl in the movie was all wrong. Mary Lennox had yellow hair. Even the book said that. And the end of the movie had kissing. That made the boys yell, "Yuck."

"Mary doesn't kiss anyone in the book," Sean complained.

"I thought it was romantic," Sonia said. "I'm glad they added it."

"Girls," Sean grumbled. "I liked it better when Mary and Colin were yelling at each other."

The discussion ended when Thomas and Kat burst through the front door and ran into the room. They shouted together, "It's snowing!"

"Really?" Sonia's eyes lit up and she raced for the window. She bumped into her brother as he scrambled over the arm of the sofa to get there first.

Meri walked to the window and looked out. Fat snowflakes fell so fast that her neighbor's house was hard to see.

"Wow, it's snowing hard," Jasmine said. "We might be here for a long time."

Meri almost groaned as her sisters followed the twins into the house, stomping snow off their feet. It looked like the worst party ever was going to drag on forever.

7

Meri and Mary Make Up

Meri's mom found mittens and scarves for Sonia and Sean to wear. Jasmine and David already had gloves in the pockets of their coats.

"Once you guys get good and wet, I want you to come in," she said. "We'll have hot chocolate."

"Yum," David said.

Meri loved snow, but she was still a little grumpy about the disaster with her mirror. She joined in a snowball fight with boys against girls. Since there were more girls with Judith joining in, they soon had splattered snowballs all over the boys.

Then they tried to make a snowman, but the snow wasn't thick enough on the ground.

They ended up with just a snow bump.

"It will probably be good snowman snow later," Meri said.

"I know," Sonia said. "Later, when we're home, we should each make a snowman and take pictures."

"Okay," Sean agreed. "But until then . . ." He scooped up more snow and splattered Sonia with it. His sister chased him around with a big handful of snow, trying to dump it down the back of his jacket.

Meri watched her friends and laughed. She still felt a little sad that she couldn't share her best secret with them, but she wasn't going to mention it again. She didn't want them to think she was weird. Still, she knew she didn't just imagine that book characters visited her. At least, she was almost sure that she knew it.

Then she remembered how Thomas had complained about her talking to her mirror. She wondered if he had heard the voices of the book characters. Maybe only people in her family could share the magic. When no one was looking, she dragged her little brother over by the shed.

"Hey, what are you doing?" Thomas complained.

"Do you remember when you thought you heard me talking to my mirror?" she said.

He rolled his eyes. "I did hear you talking to your mirror."

She waved her hand at him. "Did you hear anyone else talking? Or did you just hear me?"

"Why? Were you doing funny voices?" Thomas giggled. Meri just glared at him, until he finally sighed and said, "I only heard you."

Meri slumped. "Maybe I'm crazy," she whispered.

"Of course you are," Thomas said. "All girls are crazy."

Meri laughed a little at her brother, then let him go. He raced back to the others, and starting throwing snow. Meri slipped past her friends, expecting to hear her name called at any moment. In the thickly falling snow, no one noticed her pass by.

She climbed the porch steps and went into the house. Her mom was collecting the popcorn bowls from the living room. "In so soon?"

"Um, I have to go to the bathroom," Meri said.

Her mom nodded. "If you drip snow all over the bathroom floor, please wipe it up. Okay?"

"I will." Meri waited until her mom turned

back to the popcorn trash. Then she grabbed her copy of *The Secret Garden* from the top of the pile on the piano. She hurried upstairs with the book clutched to her chest. She stopped at the bathroom so that what she'd told her mom wouldn't be a lie. She was tired of lying.

Finally, Meri slipped into her room and put her book onto her desk. She sat in her chair and stared at the mirror. If she had been imagining, would she see Mary Lennox again?

Her curly-haired image in the mirror slowly faded and changed into Mary's thin face and long, straight yellow hair. Mary had her arms crossed as she glared out from the mirror.

"I'm so sorry I was mean to you," Meri said. "I just didn't want my friends to think I was crazy."

"Crazy is pretending something isn't there," Mary said, "when it is. When everyone at Misselthwaite Manor told me that no one was crying, I wouldn't stop saying I heard it. When they told me it was just the wind, I said it wasn't. I said it was a person. I wouldn't pretend it wasn't real."

"I know you wouldn't," Meri said sadly. "But I've only had these friends for a little while. I didn't have any friends before."

Mary tilted her head to the side. "I didn't have any friends either. I got my friends even though I insisted on telling the truth."

Then Meri remembered and pointed at the mirror. "Except about the garden," she said. "You told Colin about it like it was pretend. You didn't tell him the truth. You did exactly the same as me."

Mary took a deep breath, looking even more fierce. Then she slumped a little. "You're right. I did. I didn't like it. I didn't like telling lies."

"I don't like it either," Meri said. "But I don't know what to do. I'm the only person who can see you."

"I wonder why," Mary said.

"Maybe because it's my mirror," Meri said.

"Maybe it only works for the person who owns it."

Mary nodded slowly. "That sounds sensible. At least you can see me."

"But I can't ever share this with anyone," Meri said sadly. "I just know you'd like my friends. And they would love talking to you."

Meri heard the bang of the front door and lots of voices. "I have to go downstairs," she said quickly. "Everyone is coming in from the snow."

"Snow?" Mary said. "You have snow? I've never seen snow. It was always very hot when I was a little girl in India." She thought for a moment. "It might snow on the Moors. I don't know. I've never seen it."

"Maybe you can see the snow from the window," Meri said, pointing toward the window in the mirror room.

Mary rushed across the mirror room and pulled back the curtain. She turned back to look at Meri with a big smile. "I can see it. It's real snow!"

"Meri, what are you doing in here?" Jasmine asked. Meri turned sharply and saw Jasmine holding an armload of books.

"Um, I came up to get my copy of *The Secret Garden* for the table," she said. She felt a pain in her stomach. One more lie.

"Don't bother," Jasmine carried the pile of books over and dumped them on top of Meri's book. "Your mom said there's no room on the table for a centerpiece. She has too much food." She took hold of Meri's arm and began pulling. "We better get down there before the boys eat everything."

Meri glanced back at the mirror and Jasmine followed her head movement.

"Oh, I'm sorry about the mirror thing before," Jasmine said. "We didn't really understand what game you wanted to play. I didn't mean to make you feel bad. I know the others didn't either."

Jasmine turned to look at the mirror again.

Meri was horrified to see that Mary Lennox had walked across the room and was making faces at Jasmine.

"It's okay," Meri said. "Sometimes I get carried away. I do love the mirror. My Aunt P really did give it to me for my birthday."

"You can tell it's really old," Jasmine said, reaching out to touch the rippled glass while Mary made more faces at her.

"I like how the glass is all rippled," Jasmine

said. "It really is special."

"It really is," Meri agreed.

"So you're not mad about before?"

"No, no," Meri assured her. She wasn't really mad at her friends, not a lot anyway. All they saw was a mirror, so they couldn't believe Meri saw anything else. Still, she did wish Jasmine believed her. "You didn't even believe me a little?"

"I tried," Jasmine said. She leaned so close to the mirror that her nose nearly touched the glass. "All I see is me. Though if I look this close, I only have one eye."

Mary had clearly grown bored with making faces at Jasmine. She walked back over to the window. "You should go ahead downstairs with the others," she said. She was still standing at the window to the mirror room. "I'm going to stay here and watch the snow."

Meri gave her a small nod, then tugged on Jasmine's arm, pulling her out of the room.

Fun and Games

The wind picked up outside as Meri and her friends ate. They watched the wind blow snow against the dining room windows, making swirls and patterns on the glass.

"Snow is amazing," Sonia said. "I'm glad we had our first snowstorm here."

Meri's mom glanced at the window. "I really should call everyone's parents. If this is going to last most of the day, we might have to turn this party into a sleepover."

The whole group cheered, except for Judith. She grunted and said, "As long as I don't end up with anyone extra in my room."

"I think we can find enough spots without crowding you, Judith," her mom assured her.

"Though the bathroom wait might get longer." Judith moaned.

"Hey, the guys can sleep in my room, if they want," Thomas said eagerly. Sean and David each gave him a high five, and the little boy glowed with happiness.

Meri smiled at her little brother. He could be a pain sometimes, but he was always generous. As Meri nibbled on a cookie shaped like a flower, she thought about her conversation with Mary Lennox. Should she keep insisting her mirror was magic? Was she being a chicken by letting it go? She wanted to be fearless like Mary, but she hated having anyone mad at her. If she kept insisting, her friends might get mad. Or they might think she was too weird to hang out with.

"Thank you, Thomas," Meri's mom said. "Though we'll decide on sleeping arrangements once we know if we need any." She made a quick list of everyone's phone number so she could just go quickly down the list, then stepped out of the room to make her calls.

"I hope my mom says we can stay over," Sonia said. "I'm having so much fun."

"My mom will probably let me stay," Jasmine said. "She's so scared of driving in the snow."

"Our mom's not," Sean said. "She grew up in Minnesota. She used to tell us about snow all the time, but it's even more awesome than she said."

"Do you think we can go outside again?" David asked as he watched the snow slap the windows.

"Probably not until it stops," Meri told them. "Mom doesn't usually let us out when it's snowing and windy. It's not much fun anyway. The snow stings when the wind is blowing it in your eyes."

David nodded. "That's the worst."

A few minutes later, Meri's mom came back in. "We're sticking to the original times for going home as long as the snow stops," she said. "Except, Jasmine, your mom wants you to stay the night."

Jasmine clapped her hands. "I knew it."

"Okay, if everyone is done eating, why don't you go play an indoor game?" Meri's mom said. "We've got piles of board games in the upstairs closet."

The group thundered upstairs and poked around the game closet. "I've never seen so many games," David said.

"Some of them are for babies," Sean said.

"What's this game?" Sonia asked, pointing at an unmarked brown box.

"It's one my family made up," Meri said. "Dad bought a bunch of games at a yard sale, but they were all missing a lot of parts. So we combined them and made up our own game. It's silly."

"Let's play that one!" Sonia said as she and Sean carefully pulled the box out of the pile. They settled down on the big upstairs landing to play. When Meri pulled the big game board out of the box, everyone laughed. It was three different game boards cut apart and then taped together to make one long board.

"What are the rules?" David asked.

"Well, everyone starts at Start," Meri said. "Then you have to pick one of these cards." She pointed to a stack of old business cards. "They have different rules written on them. You have to follow the rule on your card when you take your turn. Some of the rules are kind of strange. Thomas and Kat helped write them."

They were soon caught up in the game that changed at every turn. It was hard to tell who was winning, but the silly rules soon had everyone laughing. They were so busy with the game that Meri forgot about the snow and her sad feelings about her mirror. She just had fun with her friends.

The Place to Be

Finally Meri noticed the sound of the wind howling around the house had died away. She looked up at the window above them, but she couldn't see much while sitting on the floor. The earlier blowing snow had left thick patterns of snow and frost on the glass.

"The snow stopped!" Thomas yelled from the living room.

Meri and her friends jumped up and huddled against the window to peek through the clear spots. The hours of snow had mostly filled in their footprints in the yard.

"Is it enough for a snowman?" Sonia asked.

"I think so," Meri said. "But it might be too fluffy. Fluffy snow doesn't stick together. It just puffs away."

"Fluffy snow is terrible for sledding, too," David added. "But I still think we should go out and check."

"But our gloves and stuff are so wet," Jasmine said. "We'll freeze."

"Not if I know my mom," Meri told them.

They raced downstairs and saw the soggy pile of jackets, mittens, scarves, and hats were gone from the basket next to the front door. Meri headed straight to the laundry room. Her mom looked up from the dryer, where she was pulling out jackets. She looked up and smiled. "Has it stopped snowing?"

Everyone nodded eagerly.

"Well, you better grab your stuff while it's warm," her mom said.

Everyone dived for the clothes basket at her mom's feet. Meri snagged her jacket and slipped it on. It was still warm from the dryer and felt as if she were getting a cozy hug.

It took a few minutes for everyone to sort out the mittens and gloves. Finally, they were all bundled up and toasty warm.

"Have fun," her mom called. "But watch for your parents. Some of them are coming in an hour or so."

A chorus of agreement answered as they raced for the back door. Meri stomped out, her boots breaking through the slight crust on top of the snow. In the drifts at the back steps, the snow was a little deeper than the top of her snow boots. She lifted her legs high and waded through the drift to the thinner snow of the yard.

The back hill looked like a smooth, white blanket. Meri reached down and grabbed a handful of snow at her feet. It packed tight, almost too tight to throw safely.

"It's too wet for snowballs," she said. "Someone could get hurt."

David scooped up snow and made a ball of his own. "You're right, but it's perfect snowman and sledding snow. Do you have any sleds?"

Meri nodded and pointed to the weathered outbuilding. "In the shed."

They stomped to the shed, taking high steps to keep from tripping. Finally, Meri pulled open the shed door. A pile of snow saucers lay on the floor in the corner. An old sled with runners hung from one wall next to a snowboard.

"The snowboard is Hannah's," Meri said. "So we shouldn't use it, but the saucers should work great."

Everyone grabbed a saucer and headed for the hill. "Be sure to walk up in a straight line," David said. "So we just have one walking track. That way, we don't ruin a bunch of snow for sledding."

The sledding on the hill was perfect and soon everyone was laughing and shrieking. Thomas and Kat came out soon after and demanded a turn. Meri handed over her saucer to Thomas.

"You two can share," she said. "I'm worn out. I'm going to start a snowman."

"I'll help," Jasmine said, handing her saucer to Kat. "I have enough snow down my neck for a while."

They waded to the front of the yard and began rolling snow for the snowman. When they finally had a ball big enough for the bottom of the snowman, Sonia hurried over to join them.

"Sledding is fun," she said. "But I don't want to miss out on my first snowman."

The boys held out until they were ready to make the snowman's head. Then, they both ran over. They gathered small stones from the driveway to make the snowman's face. Thomas and Kat ran over, dragging sticks for the snowman's arms.

Finally, they had a tall snowman looking out at the street. Since one eye was bigger than the other, the snowman had a questioning look as he held one stick arm high. A van pulled up next to the curb. Sonia and Sean raced toward it as their mom got out.

"Come and see our snowman," Sean said.

"Take a picture of it," Sonia insisted.

They dragged their mom closer as she tried to pick her way around the clumps of slush in the street left behind by the snowplow.

"It's beautiful," she told them. "Hey, why don't all of you gather around the snowman and I'll take your photo."

They crowded in together, everyone grinning and laughing. Meri looked around her at her snowy friends. Her party was nothing like she expected. She didn't get to share her mirror secret with one single person, but she still had great friends and a great family. The day had turned out okay after all. Even if she did feel the tiniest pull of sadness about the mirror.

She knew it was real and someday she'd figure out how to make other people see it. It was like Mary Lennox. She didn't give up when people told her no one in the big spooky house was crying. Mary believed in herself and she found Colin. Nothing in the book would have turned out right if she had quit. Meri wasn't going to quit either.

10

The Best Magic

"Mcri, smile!" Mrs. Wilson called out, pulling Meri out of her thoughts about the mirror. Meri smiled and Mrs. Wilson declared the picture, "Perfect!"

Just then, Meri's mom came out carrying goody bags for Sonia and Sean. They handed over their soggy scarves and mittens.

"We had a great time," Sonia said. "This was the best party ever." She gave Meri a quick hug.

"Yeah, it was terrific," Sean said, giving Meri a playful shove on the arm, "even if you do make up crazy stories."

"Don't start that," Sonia insisted and dragged her brother to the van.

"Hey, I wasn't complaining," Sean said. "I liked it."

Mrs. Wilson had barely pulled away from the curb before David's dad pulled up to collect him. He stayed a few minutes to admire the snowman and listen to David describe the party in a breathless rush.

"Wow, it sounds like this was the place to be today," his dad said, laughing.

"It was great," David said. He turned quickly to Meri's mom. "Thanks for letting Meri have a party."

"You're welcome," she said. "It was fun for me, too."

David looked confused. "But you didn't even go sledding."

Meri's mom laughed. "Maybe later."

When David finally left, Meri's mom turned toward Jasmine and Meri. "Do you guys want some hot chocolate?"

"Me too!" Thomas rushed up from sledding.

"Okay, but all the saucers have to go back in the shed. I'll go in and start the hot chocolate."

Meri and Jasmine followed Thomas to collect the saucers and pile them in the shed.

"This really was a great party," Jasmine said. "I'm glad it's not done yet. Do you think we could watch the other movie? I like black and white movies."

"Sure," Meri said. "My dad does too. He'll probably want to watch it after supper as a whole family."

"Super," Jasmine said.

They finished up and headed for the small enclosed back porch. They stepped out of their soggy boots and stripped off their wet outside clothes. Meri carried the pile into the house, walking right through the kitchen to the laundry room. She piled everything into a basket.

They slurped up hot chocolate as fast as they could without scalded tongues. "What's your hurry?" Meri's mom asked.

"I want to get my room ready," Meri said.

"You two won't be going to bed for hours."

"I like to get things ready early," Meri said.

"Me too," Jasmine said. "If you wait until you're tired and ready to sleep, it's not as much fun."

Meri's mom shrugged. "I guess that makes sense."

When the girls headed up to the bedroom, Meri spotted the pile of books on the desk in front of Mary Lennox. Mary was sitting at the mirror desk with her head resting on one hand.

"Oh, sorry," Meri said, then she remembered that Jasmine couldn't see Mary. "I mean, it's too bad I forgot to give everyone back their books. I guess I can take them all back to school on Monday."

"Meri," Jasmine whispered. "Who's that?"

Meri spun and stared at Jasmine. She looked very pale and pointed at the mirror. "What do you see?" Meri asked.

"A girl," Jasmine said. "But it's not you and it's not me."

Meri grinned. "You see her? You really see her?"

The girl in the mirror clapped her hands. "The magic worked after all."

"Do you mean that's Mary Lennox?" Jasmine said, her voice still soft.

"I am," Mary said.

"She is," Meri said.

"Oh." Jasmine walked forward very slowly. "Why can I see her now? I couldn't see her before."

"Maybe it just takes time," Mary suggested.

Meri looked at the desk. Her copy of *The Secret Garden* lay at the bottom of a whole pile of the books. She remembered Jasmine carrying all the books upstairs and dropping them on top of hers. "You put books on the desk," she said to Jasmine.

"I did," Jasmine said.

"When I put a book on the desk, I see the character from the book," Meri said. "But no one else does. But then you put books on the desk too. Now you can see her. Maybe that's what makes the magic work. It works for the person who puts the book there."

"Wow," Jasmine said. She looked into the mirror. "How does it feel in there? Does it feel like a real place?"

Mary nodded. "I doesn't look like any rooms at the manor. And it's warm, even though there's no fire. But it feels real, I think. I've never seen real snow out a window, but I think it's like this."

"Oh, you can see the snow?" Jasmine asked.

Mary nodded, her face lighting up. "It's beautiful. How does it feel?"

"It's a little bit soft, like mud," Jasmine said. "But not squishy like mud. It's very cold and wet. It doesn't feel the same as rain though. It doesn't feel wet until it starts to melt."

Mary was listening closely. "Have you ever tasted it? I really wanted to go out and taste snow."

"It tastes like cold," Jasmine said. "But it doesn't really have any other taste. Just cold and wet. But also soft, so not like water."

Mary's eyes looked dreamy. "I'm so glad I got to see it. In the garden, one of the trees had tiny white flowers in the spring. When the wind blew, the flowers fell. I pretended it was snow falling on me."

"We have trees like that," Jasmine said. "And some of them are pink. I pretend it's pink snow."

Mary laughed at that. "Pink snow. That would be magic."

"That's pretend magic. This is the first real magic I've ever seen," Jasmine said.

"I think there might be lots of magic," Mary said. "I have a friend who is a robin. He showed me the key to the secret garden. That was magic. And now I am talking to you right in this magic mirror."

Meri smiled as she watched her best friend talk to Mary in the mirror. She wondered if having a good friend was a kind of magic, too.

"I'm just glad I finally get to share this magic," Meri said.

Jasmine turned and looked at her with worried eyes. "Are you mad because I didn't believe you? I tried. I really did try."

"I know," Meri said. "And if you weren't my best friend, you wouldn't have tried. I'm just glad you can see it now."

Jasmine nodded, smiling. "Me too. Will you promise to tell me about all the people from the mirror?"

Meri laughed. "Promise? You'll never get me to stop!"

Then she sat down beside her friend, sharing the little chair in front of the mirror. And the three girls talked for a long time, each happy to be friends sharing the best secret in the world.

About the Author

Jan Fields grew up loving stories where exciting and slightly impossible things happened to ordinary kids like her. She still loves reading stories like that, so she writes books for children looking for the same things.

When she's not writing, Jan pokes around the New England countryside in search of inspiration, magic mirrors, and fairies.